AF223640

For those who don't always find the path easy,
who must learn in their own way, and who
refuse to stop trying.

Chapter 1

The start of another school year always brings mixed emotions.

Walking through the gates on the first day, I feel it straight away. The noise, the crowds, teachers yelling out instructions, kids comparing schedules. It's familiar, but not always in a good way. I spot Logan near the lockers and feel a bit better instantly. He grins when he sees me and punches my arm like he always does.

Break times are what I look forward to. That's when things feel normal. Basketball courts full, the sound of the ball hitting the court surface, arguments about whether a shot counted or not. That's my place. That's where my brain works.

Classrooms are different.

Sitting at a desk, staring at a book, trying to understand what the teacher is saying, it just doesn't click. English, maths, history, science... it doesn't really matter which one it is. The words might as well be written in another language. Everyone else seems to understand enough to get by. They ask questions, they write answers, they move on.

I don't.

I listen. I really do. But halfway through an explanation, I get lost, and once I'm lost, I stay lost. So, I've learned to stay quiet. I copy things down even if I don't understand them. I pretend I'm reading when I'm really just staring at the page.

So far, keeping my head down has kept me out of trouble.

Still, some days I sit there wondering why it's like this. Why school feels so hard when it doesn't seem to be for anyone else. I wonder what's wrong with me. I don't say it out loud, but the thought is always there.

This year, though, I keep telling myself it's going to be different.

Chapter 2

Logan doesn't really get why school stresses me out so much.

He's not top of the class or anything, but he understands enough to get by. He complains about homework, but he still does it. He reads questions once and somehow knows what they're asking.

I usually just nod along.

When we're together, I feel less stupid. Logan never makes me feel bad. If I don't know something, he'll explain it like it's no big deal. Or he'll just do it himself and let me copy. He doesn't say anything, and I don't ask questions.

Basketball is different. On the court, I don't need help. I know where to move, when to pass, when to shoot. I can tell how much force I need without thinking. I know when a shot feels right the moment it leaves my hands.

Teachers don't see that version of me.

They see the kid who doesn't finish work. The kid who zones out. The kid who hands in half-done assignments or doesn't hand them in at all. I've heard words like *lazy* and *unmotivated* more times than I can count.

My parents don't care to much about it so long as I'm not causing trouble they just let me be.

They don't know how hard I'm actually trying.

Most days, I just try to survive until the bell rings.

Chapter 3

Things changed late last year, in cooking class of all places.

Logan and I were partners, like always. He liked cooking class because you didn't have to write much. I liked it because we did it in pairs. Logan read the recipe and I sifted, mixed or put it in the oven.

That day, we were making cake.

Logan had already read through the recipe and started putting ingredients into the bowl. I was mixing while he talked about a game we'd played the night before. Then he said he needed to go to the toilet and told me to keep mixing.

So I did.

I mixed and mixed, trying not to panic. I knew there was a next step, but the recipe just didn't make sense to me, I couldn't work out what I needed to do. There were too many words, too many instructions. I tried to read it slowly, but nothing stuck.

I looked around the room to see what everyone else was doing. That usually helps, but we were behind, and everyone else was already ahead of us, pouring batter into cake tins.

Then I felt someone standing next to me.

Miss Reynolds.

She smiled and looked into our bowl. "Will," she said, "I think that's mixed enough. You don't need to wait for Logan. You should move on to the next step or you won't finish in time."

My chest tightened.

I didn't know what the next step was.

She must have seen it on my face, because she softened straight away. "Is everything okay?" she asked. "Do you need some help?"

"No," I said quickly, staring at the bench. "I'm fine."

I wasn't fine at all.

She didn't argue. She didn't call attention to it. She just leaned in, looked at the recipe with me, and quietly explained what to do next. One step at a time. Slowly.

Logan came back just as we were pouring the batter into the tin. He gave me a confused look, like he was trying to work out why the teacher was there. Miss Reynolds patted my shoulder and said, "Good job," before walking away.

Logan didn't ask questions.

He never does.

Chapter 4

We ate cake as the bell rang for lunch.

I was just packing my bag when Miss Reynolds came over and asked if I could meet her in her office ten minutes before lunch ended.

That's when the worry started.

On the basketball courts, I couldn't focus. I missed shots I normally make easily. Logan noticed straight away.

"You good?" he asked.

"Yeah," I said, even though I wasn't.

My phone buzzed, reminding me to go to the meeting. I made up some excuse and jogged back toward the building.

Sitting in her office felt strange. Miss Reynolds asked me to sit down. I could feel my heart pounding.

She told me straight away that I wasn't in trouble.

She said she'd noticed I might need some help and that maybe together we could come up with a plan. She said it wasn't something to be embarrassed about and that lots of kids need extra support.

I tried to deny it. I always do.

She didn't push. She just suggested checking where I was at.

I nodded.

Chapter 5

The next day, I met Mrs Miller.

Her room was quiet, and that made everything feel heavier. No Logan. No friends. Just me and the work.

She gave me some worksheets and told me to start where I could.

I stared at the page.

I honestly didn't know what to do.

It was embarrassing. Frustrating. I wanted to disappear. Mrs Miller noticed straight away and came to sit next to me. She spoke calmly, never rushed me, never made me feel like I was wasting her time.

It became clear pretty fast just how far behind I really was.

It wasn't something that I didn't already know but it still hurt all the same.

At the same time, it felt kinda nice having someone see me, and want to help.

That's how I ended up with daily lessons with Mrs Miller for Grade 9.

She knew how much I loved Basketball and obviously could see the reason I had never tried out before. She told me if I could pass my core subjects at my level, I'd be allowed to try out for the team.

Tryouts were in six weeks.

Basketball was the only thing that made sense to me.

Now there is hope, which scared me. What if I failed now, I'm not sure I could take that blow. But I decided to try anyway. Mrs Miller made me feel like it was possible.

Chapter 6

The first few weeks with Mrs Miller were harder than I expected.

At first, I thought I was doing okay. I was trying. I showed up. I listened. But the more work we did, the clearer it became just how far behind I really was. Not just a little bit behind. A lot.

Some of the reading work was stuff kids much younger than me would probably find easy. Short sentences. Simple words. Questions that should have obvious answers. Sometimes I'd read the same sentence over and over and still not know what it was saying.

Maths was worse.

Mrs Miller asked me to do basic sums in my head, things like adding and subtracting small numbers. I froze. My mind went blank. I could feel my heart beating faster, the panic closing in on me.

I hated that feeling.

One day, after I struggled through another worksheet, Mrs Miller gently explained where I was at. She didn't say it in a mean way. She didn't talk down to me. She just told me the truth.

I was working at about a primary school level, probably around grade 2.

Hearing it out loud hurt more than I expected.

I nodded like it was no big deal, but inside I felt sick. I kept thinking about everyone else my age, sitting in normal classes, doing normal work. I felt stupid. I felt like I'd been pretending for so long and now someone could finally see through it.

I went quiet after that.

Mrs Miller noticed straight away.

She told me being behind
didn't mean I couldn't
move forward, some
people just learn different
and that maybe we just
needed to find a different
way to look at thing.

She said everyone starts from somewhere, and
what mattered was that I was willing to try. I
didn't really believe her at first. It felt like she
was just saying what teachers are supposed to
say.

But she didn't give up on me.

Instead of pushing harder, she slowed things
down. She broke work into smaller pieces. She
explained things more than once without
getting annoyed. When I got something wrong,
she didn't say *wrong*. She just asked me to try it
another way.

Still, there were days I left her room feeling
exhausted.

Some afternoons, I went straight to the basketball courts with Logan and just shot until my arms hurt. On the court, everything felt normal again. I didn't have to think. I just played.

One day, Mrs Miller asked me how many points a three-pointer was worth.

"Three," I said instantly.

She smiled.

Then she asked, "If you make four three-pointers, how many points is that?"

"Twelve," I answered without even thinking.

She paused for a second, then slid a maths sheet toward me. Instead of random numbers, it had basketball scores written on it. Points. Fouls. Quarters. Time left on the clock.

For the first time, the numbers didn't feel pointless.

I wasn't good at it yet. Not even close.

But I wasn't completely lost either.

And that was new.

Chapter 7

By the time lunch rolled around each day, my head usually felt full.

Not full in a good way. More like tired. Mrs Miller's lessons took a lot out of me. Even when I tried hard, it felt like my brain was working twice as hard as it should.

That's why lunch time mattered so much.

The moment the bell rang, Logan and I headed straight for the courts. The noise followed us, laughing, shouting, shoes squeaking, the ball slapping against the concrete. It felt familiar. Safe.

Logan tossed me the ball.
"First to five?" he said.

I nodded.

As soon as the ball was in my hands, everything else faded. No worksheets. No words I couldn't understand. Just the court, the hoop, and the rhythm of the game.

I didn't miss.

Not once.

Three after three dropped clean through the net. The sound of it was perfect. Swish. Swish. Swish. Logan laughed and shook his head.

"Man, that's not fair," he said. "You're automatic."

I didn't say anything. I didn't need to. This was the one place where I didn't feel behind. Where I didn't feel like I was pretending.

A couple of other boys joined in. Then a couple more. We started playing half-court, calling fouls, keeping score in our heads. I always knew where we were at. Eleven to eight. Thirteen to eleven.

Counting points like this felt easy. Natural.

If someone hit a three pointer, I instantly knew the new score. If someone got fouled and made both free throws, that was two more points. No thinking required.

At one point, Logan missed a shot and I grabbed the rebound, stepped back behind the line, and shot without hesitating.

Swish.

"Game," Logan said.

I jogged off the court, breathing hard but smiling. My arms felt good. Strong.

For a moment, I wished school could feel like this. Clear. Simple. Like there was always a right move if you just knew the game well enough.

When the bell rang to head back to class, the feeling faded. Just a bit.

But it stayed with me longer than usual.

And for the first time, I wondered if maybe, just maybe school could start to make sense too.

Chapter 8

After school, I didn't go straight home like I usually did.

Logan had to catch the bus, but I stayed back at the courts with a ball under my arm. The air was cooler, and the courts were mostly empty. I liked it that way. No pressure. No noise. Just me and the hoop.

I started close to the basket, taking easy shots. Layups. Bank shots. Nothing fancy. Then I stepped back. Free-throw line. Baseline. Three-point line.

I kept shooting.

Each shot felt the same. Catch. Bend my knees. Release. Follow through.

I didn't think about school. I didn't think about Mrs Miller or worksheets or how far behind I was. I just focused on the ball and the rim.

Swish.

Swish.

I didn't notice anyone watching me.

I was so focused that I didn't hear footsteps until a voice spoke from behind me.

"Nice shot."

I turned around fast, my heart jumping a little.

It was Mr Smit. The basketball coach.

He stood near the edge of the court, hands in his pockets, watching me with a small smile. I felt awkward straight away. I wasn't doing anything wrong, but it still felt strange being watched.

"Thanks," I said, wiping my hands on my shorts.

He asked me how long I'd been playing for. Asked what year I was in. Normal stuff. Then he asked something that caught me off guard.

"Ever thought about trying out for the school team?"

I hesitated.

I told him the truth. That I wanted to. That I always had. But that I hadn't been allowed to before because of my schoolwork.

He nodded slowly, like that made sense.

"Well," he said, "I've been noticing you out here at lunch. You've got good form. Good control."

I didn't know what to say to that.

Before he left, he told me to keep working. Said tryouts were coming up fast. Said effort mattered as much as talent.

When I finally walked home, the ball tucked under my arm, my head was spinning.

Someone had noticed.

And this time, it wasn't for the wrong reasons.

Chapter 9

The next day in Mrs Miller's room, I couldn't stop thinking about what Mr Smit had said.

Nice shot.
Ever thought about trying out?

I kept replaying it in my head while Mrs Miller talked me through a reading task. I was there, but I wasn't really there. She noticed pretty quickly.

"You seem distracted today," she said gently.

I shrugged. "Just tired."

She didn't push, but after a moment she slid my maths book aside and pulled out a different sheet. This one had a basketball court printed on it, with numbers written around the key and the three-point line.

My attention snapped back straight away.

"We're going to try something a bit different," she said. "Tell me what you see."

I leaned forward without thinking. "That's the three-point line. That spot's the top of the key."

She smiled. "Okay. So if you make two shots from here" she pointed beyond the arc "how many points do you score?"

"Three."

"And if you miss one but get fouled and make both free throws?"

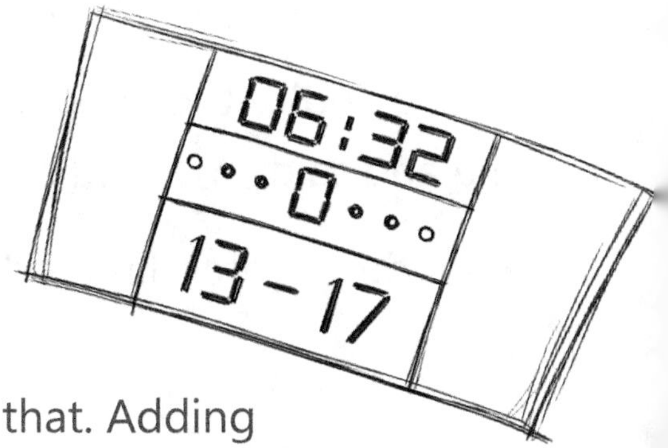

"Two."

She nodded like she expected that answer.

We started working through problems like that. Adding points. Subtracting scores. Working out totals at the end of a quarter.

She even asked me how long a game was and how many minutes were in each quarter. I had to stop and think about that one, but I got there.

For the first time, I wasn't guessing.

When we moved back to reading, she handed me a short paragraph about basketball rules. Travelling. Double dribble. Fouls. Stuff I already understood, just written down instead of spoken.

I still had to read it slowly. I still stumbled over some words. But I didn't feel completely lost.

At the end of the lesson, Mrs Miller looked at me and said, "You did good work today, Will."

I nodded, pretending it didn't matter.

But it did.

Later that day, Logan caught up with me near the lockers.

"You staying back again?" he asked.

"Yeah," I said.

He grinned. "Mum's picking me up today I've got 20 minutes lets go"

Walking toward the courts, I felt something new settling in my chest.

Not confidence exactly.

But belief.

Chapter 10

A few days later, Mrs Miller told me someone else would be joining our lesson.

I didn't like the sound of that.

I sat there waiting, tapping my pencil against the desk, trying not to think about what it could mean. When the door opened and Mr Smit walked in, my stomach flipped.

He smiled when he saw me. "Hey, Will."

Mrs Miller gestured for him to sit down. "Mr Smit and I have been talking," she said. "About ways we can help you."

I felt my shoulders tense straight away.

I waited for them to say something bad. That I wasn't improving fast enough. That tryouts were off.

Instead, they started talking about basketball.

Mr Smit explained the rules in detail. How scoring works. How fouls affect the game. How time on the clock changes decisions. Mrs Miller listened, asking questions, writing notes.

Then she turned to me.

"If we use basketball to help explain things," she said, "does that make it easier?"

I nodded without thinking. "Yeah."

So that's what we did.

Maths became about keeping score, averages, and percentages. How many shots I made out of ten. How that turned into a percentage. How long a possession lasted if the shot clock was running down.

English became reading short texts about basketball. Writing simple summaries of games. Explaining rules in my own words.

Even science came into it. Mr Smit talked about angles and force, about how the ball needed the right arc to drop through the hoop. Mrs

Miller turned that into questions I could actually understand.

For the first time, school didn't feel like something being done *to* me.

It felt like something I was part of.

When the lesson ended, Mr Smit clapped me lightly on the shoulder. "Keep working," he said. "You've got this."

As I walked to my next class, I realised something.

I was actually looking forward to coming back to school tomorrow.

Chapter 11

School started to feel different after that.

Not suddenly. Not all at once. Just in small ways that were hard to explain.

I still struggled. I still had moments where words didn't make sense and numbers swam around on the page. But I wasn't completely stuck anymore. When something didn't click straight away, Mrs Miller didn't move on. She stayed with it until I understood enough to keep going.

A lot of our work still connected back to basketball.

We used game scores to practise adding and subtracting. We worked out averages from shooting drills. Sometimes she'd ask me to explain a rule out loud first, then help me write it down in simple sentences. Writing was still hard, but at least I knew what I wanted to say.

Slowly, she started changing things.

Instead of basketball scores, we used other numbers. Instead of basketball rules, we read short stories that had nothing to do with sport. At first, that threw me off. I didn't like it. It felt like the safety net was being pulled away.

Mrs Miller noticed.

She told me it was okay to feel uncomfortable. That the goal wasn't to stay in basketball forever, but to use it to build skills I could use anywhere. I didn't fully get it, but I trusted her enough to keep trying.

Outside of class, things were changing too.

Basketball training had started; tryouts were getting closer. Coach Smit ran conditioning sessions after school, and I pushed

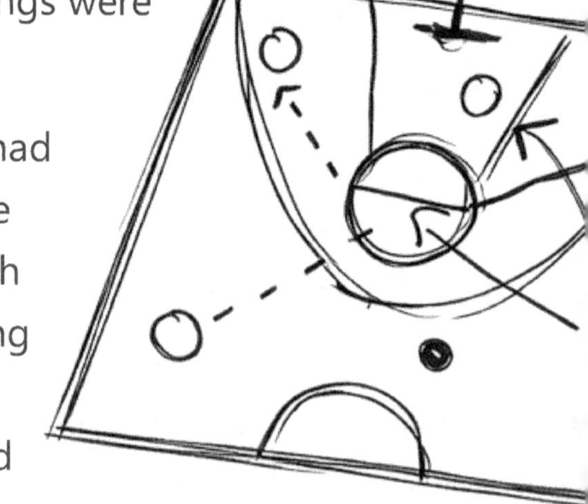

myself harder than ever. Some nights I went home exhausted, my legs aching, my arms heavy.

Logan was always there, cracking jokes, complaining about drills, daring me to take stupid shots during breaks. Being on the court with him made everything feel lighter.

For the first time, I felt like school and basketball weren't fighting each other.

They were starting to work together.

Chapter 12

Training sessions started to heat they were after school, three afternoons a week, and they were nothing like playing at lunch. Coach Smit didn't mess around. We ran drills over and over. Passing. Footwork. Defence. Shooting under pressure.

At first, I was worried I wouldn't keep up.

But once we started playing, my body knew what to do. I moved without thinking. I passed when someone was open. When I shot, my form stayed solid, even when I was tired.

Coach Smit noticed.

He didn't say much, but every now and then he nodded or called out my name during drills. That was enough. It told me I was doing something right.

The harder part was everything else.

By the time I got home after training, I was exhausted. Some nights I fell asleep still thinking about drills, about plays, about the sound of the ball hitting the court. The next morning, sitting in class, my eyes felt heavy and my head felt slow.

Mrs Miller noticed that too.

I struggled more on those days. Made careless mistakes. Lost focus quicker than usual. It scared me. I didn't want to slip back. I didn't want to give anyone a reason to say I couldn't try out.

Mrs Miller reminded me to slow down. To take breaks. To keep doing the small things that were helping me improve. She said progress didn't disappear just because I had a bad day.

Tryouts were getting closer.

Coach Smit mentioned it at the end of one session. "One week to go," he said. "Make it count."

That night, I lay in bed staring at the ceiling.

I thought about the court.
I thought about school.
I thought about how close I was to something I'd wanted for a long time.

I didn't know how tryouts would go.

But I felt hopeful.

Chapter 13

The day of tryouts didn't feel real when I woke up.

It felt like any other school day at first. Same uniform. Same bag. Same walk through the gates. But everything felt heavier. My chest was tight, and my stomach felt off, like I'd forgotten something important.

By the time I got to Mrs Miller's room, my head was already somewhere else.

She noticed straight away.

I kept rereading the same sentence, losing my place every time. The numbers on the page blurred together. I tapped my foot under the desk without meaning to.

"You're not here today," she said gently.

I shrugged. "Tryouts."

She nodded like she expected that answer.

She didn't tell me to calm down. She didn't tell me it would be fine. She just slid the work aside and talked me through my breathing. Slow. Steady. Like we'd done before when things felt too much.

"You've done the work," she said. "Today isn't about proving anything. It's about playing the way you know how to play."

The bell rang not long after.

At lunch, the courts were already busy. Coach Smit stood near the sideline with a clipboard. A few boys were stretching. Others were shooting around, trying to look relaxed.

I didn't feel relaxed at all.

My hands felt stiff when I caught the ball. My first few shots were short. One bounced off the rim completely. I heard someone laugh and felt my face burn.

someone laugh and felt my face burn.

Logan jogged over. "You're fine," he said quietly. "Just play."

I nodded, even though my legs felt shaky.

Then we started running drills.

Passing first. Then defence. Then shooting under pressure.

Something shifted.

My body took over before my brain could get in the way. I stopped thinking about who was watching. I stopped thinking about missing. I focused on the ball, the space, the timing.

Shots started to fall.

I hit one from the corner. Then another from the wing. When we scrimmaged, I moved like I always did at lunch, cutting, passing, taking the open shot when it was there.

By the end, my lungs were burning and sweat dripped down my back.

But I was smiling.

For the first time that day, I wasn't scared anymore.

I'd shown up.

And I felt like I had done enough.

Chapter 14

Waiting turned out to be worse than tryouts.

Coach Smit told us the list would be up the next day. That was it. No hints. No comments. Just wait.

That afternoon felt endless. In class, I stared at the clock more than the page. Every time someone laughed or whispered, I wondered if they knew something I didn't.

Logan didn't say much either.

That wasn't like him.

We went to the courts at lunch, but neither of us played properly. Shots bounced out. Passes were sloppy. My mind wasn't on the game.

"What if I don't make it?" I said finally.

Logan stopped dribbling. "Then we deal with it," he said. "But you played well. You know that."

I wanted to believe him.

The next morning, the list was taped to the noticeboard outside the gym.

A crowd had already formed by the time we got there. Boys pushed forward, scanning names, calling out to each other. My heart pounded so hard I could feel it in my ears.

I stood back at first, afraid to look.

Logan grabbed my arm. "Come on."

We pushed through together.

I ran my finger down the list slowly. My eyes jumped over names I recognised, names I didn't.

Then I saw it.

Will H.

For a second, I wasn't sure it was real.

Then Logan yelled my name, loud enough for half the hall to hear. He slapped my back and laughed like he'd won something himself.

I just stood there, staring at the paper.

I'd made the squad.

We both had.

Later that day, Coach Smit told us there were two weeks of intense training before games started. He said commitment mattered now more than ever.

Walking home, my legs felt light.

I knew it wasn't the end of the work.

But it was the start of something I'd never thought I'd reach.

Chapter 15

The two weeks of training started straight away.

Coach Smit wasn't easing us into anything. Every session was hard. We ran until our legs burned. We practised plays over and over until everyone knew where they were meant to be without thinking.

I loved it.

But it took more out of me than I expected.

By the time I got home after training, I was wrecked. Some nights I barely ate before falling asleep. In the mornings, my body felt heavy, like it hadn't fully recovered yet.

At school, it started to show.

I found it harder to focus in Mrs Miller's lessons. My eyes drifted. I made mistakes on work I'd been getting better at. A few times, I caught myself staring out the window, thinking about drills instead of numbers.

Mrs Miller of course noticed straight away.

"You're tired," she said.

I nodded. There wasn't much point pretending.

She reminded me why all of this mattered. That basketball was important, but so was the work that allowed me to be there in the first place. She didn't threaten me or scare me. She just made it clear that if I stopped trying, everything could slip.

That scared me enough.

I started paying more attention to how I looked after myself. I went to bed earlier. I ate properly, even when I didn't feel like it. I used breaks to rest instead of shooting every spare minute.

Logan helped too.

When I started zoning out, he nudged me. When I complained about being tired, he reminded me why we were doing this.

The work didn't get easier.

But I didn't give up.

Chapter 16

The first game was getting closer.

Training stayed intense, but it started to feel more focused. We worked on plays we'd actually use. Coach Smit talked more about teamwork and less about conditioning. That made it feel real. Like this wasn't just practice anymore.

At school, things were holding steady.

I wasn't flying through work or anything, but I  wasn't slipping either. Mrs Miller checked in with me more often. Sometimes she'd just ask how tired I was, or how training was going. It helped knowing someone was paying attention.

One afternoon, Coach Smit pulled me aside after training.

I thought I'd done something wrong.

Instead, he asked how school was going.

I told him the truth. That it was hard. That I was trying. That I didn't want to mess this up.

He nodded and said he'd been talking to the principal. Said as long as I kept improving and stayed committed, I'd be allowed to stay on the team.

Hearing that made my chest feel tight.

It wasn't a free pass. It was a chance.

When I told Mrs Miller the next day, she smiled in a way that made me think she already knew.

"Just keep doing what you're doing," she said. "That's all anyone can ask."

Walking to class after that, I felt nervous.

But it wasn't the bad kind.

It was the kind that meant something mattered.

Chapter 17

Game day felt different from the moment I woke up.

I didn't feel sick or panicked like I had on tryout day. Instead, there was this tight feeling in my chest that wouldn't go away. Like energy with nowhere to go.

At school, I couldn't stop thinking about the game. Even in Mrs Miller's class, my eyes kept drifting to the clock. She noticed, but this time she didn't say much. Just gave me a look that said *you've got this*.

After school, we met in the change rooms.

The air smelled like sweat and deodorant. Everyone was louder than usual, trying to act relaxed. Logan sat next to me, lacing up his shoes.

"First game," he said. "Feels weird, hey?"

I nodded.

When we ran out onto the court, the noise hit me straight away. Shoes squeaking. Balls bouncing. Voices echoing around the gym. Our rivals were already warming up on the other side.

The game started fast.

I didn't play much in the first quarter. When I did get on, my hands felt stiff again. I missed my first shot. Then my second. Coach Smit didn't yell. He just told me to keep moving.

By the second half, things slowed down.

I started to find space. Made a clean pass. Grabbed a rebound. Hit a mid-range shot. Nothing special, but it helped.

The score stayed close the whole game.

With seconds left on the clock, we were down by two.

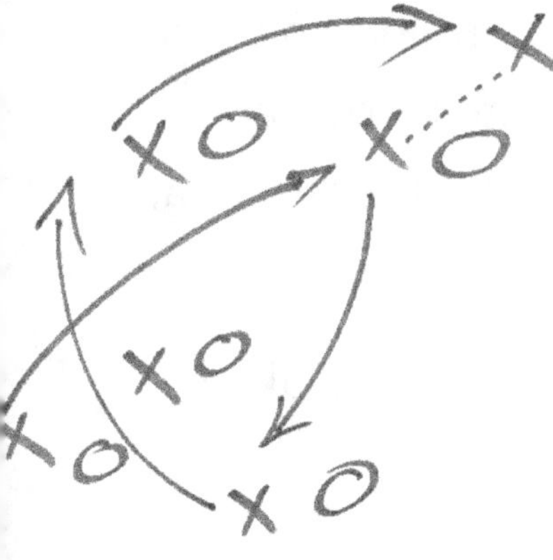

Coach Smit called a timeout.

He drew up a simple play. Nothing fancy. The ball swung around the key, and if the defence collapsed, I'd be open on the wing waiting just beyond the tree point arc.

When the whistle blew, everything went quiet in my head.

The pass came.

I didn't hesitate.

I shot.

The ball left my hands and felt right straight away.

Swish.

The buzzer sounded.

We won.

Logan tackled me in a hug, laughing and yelling at the same time. My teammates crowded around, slapping my back. I could barely hear anything over the noise.

Walking off the court, my legs were shaking.

Not from fear, but pure joy.

Being a part of the team meant everything to me.

Chapter 18

The next day at school, everything felt a little different.

People talked about the game in the halls. A few kids nodded at me or said "nice shot" as they passed. I didn't really know how to respond. I just nodded back and kept walking.

In Mrs Miller's class, I sat down like usual, but my head was still buzzing.

She didn't start the lesson straight away. She waited until the room was quiet, then looked at me.

"So," she said, "how did it go?"

I smiled before I could stop myself. "We won."

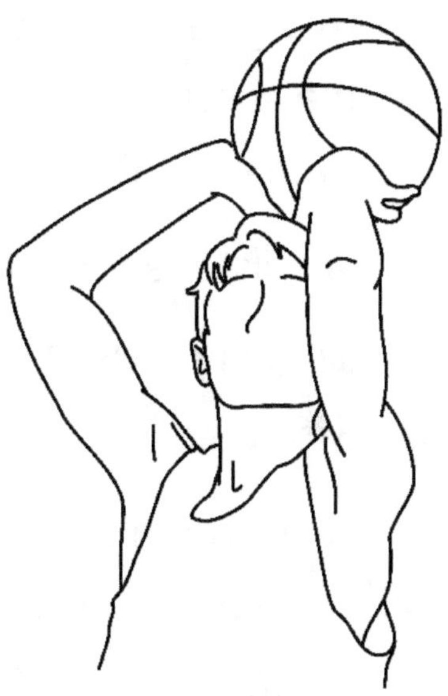

She smiled too, but she didn't say anything else. She just waited.

That's when it all came out.

I told her how scared I'd been last year. How pretending not to care about basketball had been easier than admitting how badly I wanted it. How every time someone talked about the team, it felt like a reminder of something I wasn't allowed to have.

I told her how tired I'd been. How hard it was trying to keep up with school and training at the same time. How some days I still felt stupid, even though I knew I was improving.

She listened without interrupting.

When I finished, she said something that stuck with me.

"You weren't lazy," she said. "You were protecting yourself."

I hadn't thought about it like that before.

She told me she was proud of the work I'd put in. Not just the basketball, but the effort I showed every day, even when it was hard.

Before the bell rang, she reminded me that this wasn't the end. That one game didn't change everything, and neither did one good year.

But walking out of her room, I felt lighter than I had in a long time.

I didn't feel like I was pretending anymore.

Chapter 19

The rest of the year didn't suddenly become easy.

There were still bad days. Days where school felt heavy again. Days where I mixed things up or forgot steps or needed Mrs Miller to explain something more than once. But the difference was, I didn't shut down like I used to.

I kept trying.

Basketball season rolled on, game after game. Some I played well in, some I didn't. We lost a few. We won most. Logan and I got better at reading each other on the court. We didn't even need to talk half the time. I knew where he'd be, and he knew when I was about to shoot.

At school, I kept working with Mrs Miller every day.

The work slowly changed. It wasn't always about basketball anymore. Sometimes it was just reading a short story and answering questions. Sometimes it was maths problems that had nothing to do with scores or courts or games.

I still struggled.

But I understood more than I used to.

Near the end of the year, Mrs Miller sat me down and showed me my progress. She explained it carefully, the same way she always did.

I'd gone up about four grade levels.

Hearing that didn't make me feel smart.

It made me feel proud.

The last basketball game of the season was the championship. The gym was packed. The game was tight the whole way through. We played hard, trusted each other, and didn't panic when things went wrong.

When the final buzzer sounded, we'd won.

Logan yelled. Coach Smit smiled like he was trying not to. I just stood there for a second, letting it all sink in.

Chapter 20

The last week of school felt different to the rest of the year.

Classes were winding down. Teachers weren't piling on work anymore. Lockers were half empty, and people were already talking about holidays and next year. It felt strange walking through the halls knowing it was almost over.

That afternoon, our yearbooks were handed out.

I didn't think much of it at first. I flipped through mine slowly, stopping at photos of classes and random school events. Most of it felt familiar but distant, like it had happened to someone else.

Then I found the spread on the basketball team.

There we were, lined up in our uniforms. Logan was standing next to me, grinning like always. I looked different than I remembered feeling at the start of the year. Standing taller. Belonging there.

I stared at that photo for a long time.

At the start of the year, I never would have imagined myself in it. Back then, being on the team felt impossible. I'd told myself it didn't matter. That I didn't care. But seeing the proof right there on the page made something settle in my chest.

I'd done that.

Not just the basketball.

I thought about Mrs Miller's room. The worksheets that scared me at first. The days I wanted to give up. The small wins that added up over time. Being able to read things on my own now. Doing maths without my mind going blank straight away.

I still had a long way to go. I knew that.

But I'd moved forward. A lot.

On the last day of school, I walked out through the gates with my yearbook tucked under my arm. Logan walked beside me, already talking about next season and what we could work on over the break.

I looked back at the building once before we left.

I wasn't the same kid who walked in at the start of the year.

I still had work to do.
Still so many things to learn.

But I felt proud of myself and the year I finally got my chance.